For Maria and Ness
N. W.

To Felix and Oscar
P. B.

First published in Great Britain in 2004 by
Chrysalis Children's Books
An imprint of Chrysalis Books Group plc
The Chrysalis Building, Bramley Road
London W10 6SP
www.chrysalisbooks.co.uk
This edition distributed by Publishers Group West.

Text © Nick Ward 2004
Illustrations © Peter Bailey 2004
Design and layout © Chrysalis Children's Books 2004

Designed by Sarah Goodwin

A CIP catalogue record for this book is available
from the British Library.

ISBN 1 84458 038 5

Set in Bembo
Printed in China

2 4 6 8 10 9 7 5 3 1

This book can be ordered direct from the publisher. Please contact
the Marketing Department. But try your bookshop first.

The Ice Child

Nick Ward

Illustrated by Peter Bailey

Chrysalis Children's Books

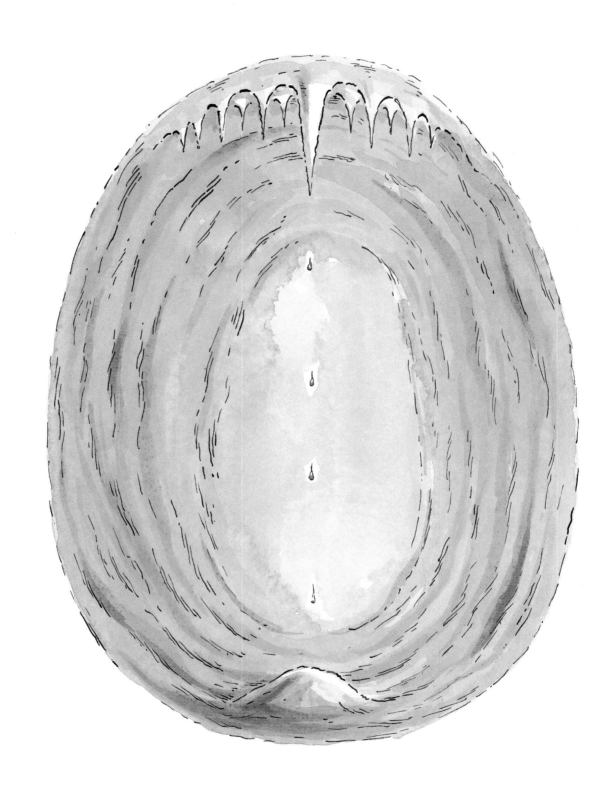

Deep in a lonely cavern, across a wasteland of ice and snow, in the heart
of the frozen north, an icicle started to drip ... drip ... drip.

As each drop of water landed on the cavern floor below, it froze once again.
A hump of ice began to form. Slowly the icicle dripped
and slowly the mound got bigger.

For ten years its shape shifted and changed until it had taken the form
of a child. Then one dark morning the sky burst in a crash of thunder.
The figure shivered and cracked ... and the ice child was born.

His home was the cavern, desolate and cold, and there the ice child stayed, completely alone. Then one day as he looked out of his cavern, he saw something move on the frozen landscape. He followed a trail of smoke to the edge of the sea where a fishing boat rocked gently at the water's edge.

The captain and his crew sang a shanty as they repaired their nets. Still as silence, the ice child stood and watched.

The captain looked up and shivered.

"Good heavens," he gasped, walking over to the child. "Where did you come from?"

The ice child pointed toward the cave. The captain sent his men to look for the boy's family, but of course they could find no one.

"You'd better come with us," the captain smiled, wrapping his jacket around the boy's icy shoulders. Together they boarded the boat and set sail.

As the fishing boat steered through the swelling sea, the captain spoke kindly to the boy. But the boy was unused to kindness, and the captain's warm words stung his cold ears. Stretching out a hand, the boy touched the captain's chest with his finger. It froze his heart in an instant, and from that moment the captain changed.

A storm blew up and the waves grew bigger and wilder.

"Captain!" yelled the first mate above the noise of the storm, "We must turn about. There's a ship in distress."

"Leave it," growled the captain. "Let someone else go. We'll miss the market and our catch will be ruined."

The crew were amazed. They had never known their captain to be so cold-hearted. But no one dared argue and they headed for home.

As the storm clouds parted, they arrived at the busy fishing village. The captain began to scan the dock for his daughter, but then he remembered she had been ill with a fever and would be waiting for him at home. He smiled as he thought of her, but his icy heart froze the smile on his lips, and the captain turned toward the market instead of home.

Left alone, the ice child walked through the bustling streets.
It was the day of the village festival, and the brightness of the
bunting and flowers were strange to the ice child's eyes.
Happy voices rang out all around and confused him.

A line of happy children danced through the crowds. Half-scared, half-curious, the ice child followed them into a big hall. The children crowded round the odd-looking boy and stared. Their curious eyes seemed to burn right through his pearly ice skin, making it tingle and prickle. Nervous now, the ice boy blew a frosty breath into the air. At once a million brilliant patterns covered the tall windows.

The children gasped in wonder and fear.

"Who are you?" one asked.

"Where do you come from?" said another.

They jostled and pushed and the ice child panicked. He turned and ran. Whooping and calling, the children chased after him, up a wide stone staircase and out through the ice-patterned doors to a balcony.

With eyes wide and glazed with fear, the ice child surveyed the noisy village spread out below. His skin frosted, the air around grew misty as it chilled and the children were frozen, solid as statues.

Gradually the mist spread out across the village. Rooftops became covered in sheets of white, flowers frosted and died. The leaves on the trees withered and fell. As the air chilled, the villagers froze. Not a sound broke the icy silence. Feeling safe now, the ice child hurried away.

In a house overlooking the harbor, a young girl watched for her father.
A slight fever still flushed her cheeks and beaded her brow, and as the ice boy's
freeze rolled over the village, she alone remained unaffected. As the chilling mist
swirled through the streets, the girl became alarmed. She rushed downstairs
to find her old nurse, but she had been turned to ice.

The girl gasped in fear and, wrapping a coat around her shoulders, she opened the door, desperate to find her father. But there on the path stood the ice child.

The young girl looked into the stranger's glacial eyes and shivered. Shocked, she stepped back into the house. The ice boy followed.

He felt the heat of her gaze and a liquid shudder swept through him, so he reached out to freeze her with his icy fingers. He touched her but nothing happened.

"Who are you. What's happening?" the girl demanded in a sudden rush of hot temper.

The ice child clapped his hands. A thousand shards of ice exploded in the air and rained down on the girl, but once more nothing happened. The ice child started to panic, and the girl realized that he was frightened and alone.

Her face softened into a smile. "Don't be scared," she said. "We can be friends."

The ice child's chest flushed with a painful warmth. He put his hand out once more to try and freeze her, but the girl took and held his hand in hers.

"Where do you come from?" she asked kindly.

The ice child felt the heat from her hand and knew he had to stop her, to stop the hot little pulses of electricity that were dancing through his limbs.

He was safe in his icy loneliness; he must never melt.

The ice boy crackled. His anger started as a chill wind, then whipped itself up into an icy storm. Soon a great blizzard lashed around the room, but the little girl seemed unconcerned.

The ice boy threw out his hands. Needles of hail flew out like a whirlwind. The air howled and as the ice storm reached its peak, the girl felt her fever cool. She smiled and, as the storm abated, the room filled with sun.

The ice boy looked at the little girl. He was very still.

His fingers tingled and his eyes smarted.

Little rivers of water streaked his face.

His chest started to heave.

And he cried his little ice heart right out.

The ice child was gone, and in his place stood a real live boy.

"Ah, there you are," said the girl. "Now perhaps you will tell me your story."

The boy felt his warm new heart start to beat. As life pumped through his limbs, he threw back his head and let out a full-blooded yell of joy. The cry echoed through the frozen village; the ice cracked, the air warmed and the village woke as if from a deep sleep.

Hand in hand, the two children rushed into the garden.

Flowers burst back into bloom, leaves sprouted from the trees' twiggy fingers. The comforting sound of the girl's nurse, busy again in the kitchen, drifted from an open window. The boy told the story of his icy home in the bleak frozen wastelands of the north, and of the kindly captain who had helped him.

Just then the captain himself pushed open the garden gate.

"Daddy!" cried the girl and rushed into his open arms.

"You look better!" laughed the captain. Then he saw the boy and his face hardened. "So this is where you got to," he said coldly.

"Can he stay?" asked his daughter. "He has nowhere to go."

The captain looked warily at the boy, and as the child reached out he grabbed his hand to stop its icy chill.

But this time the captain felt a new warmth flood through him from the boy's fingers, and he smiled. "Of course he must stay," he said.